VENICE

ALY

ORPHANAGE

PALACE

MAP
NOT TO SCALE.
INDIA MUCH MUCH MUCH
MUCH MUCH FURTHER
AWAY!

FOR ELLIE – HW

FOR HARRIET – BM

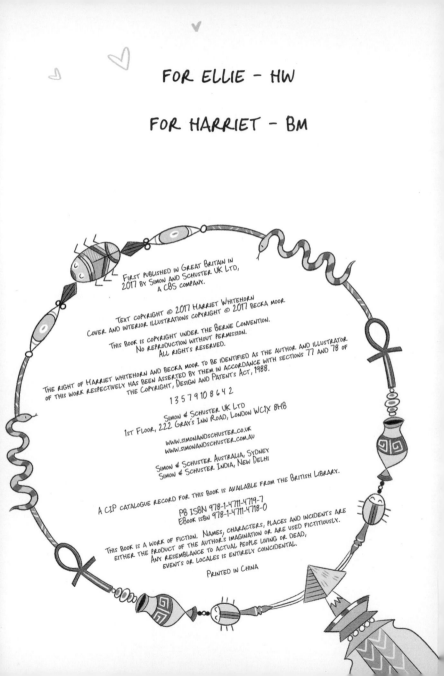

First published in Great Britain in
2017 by Simon and Schuster UK Ltd,
A CBS company.

Text copyright © 2017 Harriet Whitehorn
Cover and interior illustrations copyright © 2017 Becka Moor

1 3 5 7 9 10 8 6 4 2

Simon & Schuster UK Ltd
1st Floor, 222 Gray's Inn Road, London WC1X 8HB

www.simonandschuster.co.uk
www.simonandschuster.com.au

Simon & Schuster Australia, Sydney
Simon & Schuster India, New Delhi

A CIP catalogue record for this book is available from the British Library.

PB ISBN 978-1-4711-4719-7
EBook ISBN 978-1-4711-4718-0

Printed in China

This is a story about Violet Remy-Robinson.

Violet lives with her parents, Camille and Benedict, as well as her cat, Pudding, and her cockatoo, the Maharani. Her home is a flat that backs onto a large garden, called a communal garden, which is shared by all the people who live in the houses around it. Violet's special friends who live there are Rose and Art and Art's great-aunt, an eccentric lady called Dee Dee Derota.

Violet is always on the lookout for a mystery and, together with Rose and Art, she has already solved three crimes – the theft of an expensive jewel that belonged to Dee Dee, the kidnapping of the cockatoo who now lives with her, the Maharani, and last year, when the three friends were on holiday in Venice, they even helped catch a gang of smugglers! In each of these cases, they had a little help from a policeman called PC Green. (Very little, Violet would say, although PC Green may say differently.)

Now, as you may have guessed from the title, this book is about mummies and all things Ancient Egyptian, so I thought I would introduce you to the main characters in the story by telling you their favourite Ancient Egyptian fact.

VIOLET

DOLORES

THE ANCIENT EGYPTIAN CIVILISATION BEGAN OVER 5000 YEARS AGO AND ENDED IN 30BC, WHEN THE KINGDOM WAS CONQUERED BY THE ROMANS.

ANCIENT EGYPTIAN KINGS WERE CALLED PHARAOHS. THE MOST FAMOUS PHARAOH TODAY IS THE BOY KING TUTANKHAMUN, WHOSE TOMB WAS DISCOVERED IN 1922, FULL OF AMAZING TREASURE.

ROSE

COUSIN AGNES

THE ANCIENT EGYPTIANS INVENTED A SYSTEM OF WRITING CALLED HIEROGLYPHICS, WHICH USES PICTURES (KNOWN AS HIEROGLYPHS) INSTEAD OF WORDS.

TUTANKHAMUN'S STEPMOTHER, QUEEN NEFERTITI, IS ALSO VERY FAMOUS. HER TOMB HAS NEVER BEEN FOUND.

ART

PC GREEN

THE PYRAMIDS WERE TOMBS FOR THE PHARAOHS WHO LIVED IN THE CENTURIES BEFORE TUTANKHAMUN. BUT, BY THE TIME TUTANKHAMUN DIED, PHARAOHS WERE BURIED IN THE VALLEY OF THE KINGS, NEAR LUXOR.

PROFESSOR FITZHERBERT

THE ANCIENT EGYPTIANS BELIEVED IN LIFE AFTER DEATH, SO PRESERVED THE BODIES OF THEIR DEAD AS MUMMIES.

TUTANKHAMUN AND NEFERTITI LIVED IN THE PERIOD OF HISTORY THAT'S CALLED THE NEW KINGDOM. IT WAS FROM THE SIXTEENTH CENTURY BC TO THE ELEVENTH CENTURY BC.

It all began on a miserable, wet and cold January afternoon.

It was just the sort of weather that makes you want to curl up and eat warm, buttery crumpets and drink hot chocolate, so you will be pleased to hear that is exactly what Violet was doing. She was sitting in her cosy kitchen, after a very dull day at school and a soaking-wet walk home with her best friend, Rose, and she was trying to warm up

and cheer up. Pudding, Violet's cat, was on her knee, hoping a bit of crumpet would miss Violet's mouth and end up in his. And the Maharani, Violet's cockatoo, was perched by the window, surveying the wintry weather with disgust.

'Did you see the postcards for you?' Norma, the Remy-Robinsons' housekeeper, asked.

Violet shook her head and Norma handed them to her.

The first was a picture of a bright red sports car and, when she turned it over, her godfather, Johnny, had written on the back, *Your First Car?!*

Violet giggled. At Christmas, she had spent

a very jolly week in Dorset with her parents, Benedict and Camille, and Johnny and his wife Elena. They had stayed in a cottage that was at the end of a long dirt track. Much to Camille's disapproval, Johnny and Benedict had taught Violet how to drive a car. She had loved it, almost as much as playing poker, which Johnny had taught her when she was very little, and they always had a game when they were together.

The other postcard had a picture of an Egyptian mummy on the front, with the words, **'Greetings from the Museum of Egyptian Antiquities, Cairo'**. As you may know, Cairo is the capital city of Egypt and,

although Violet had never been there, she knew all about the museum, because it was where her Aunt Matilde, Camille's sister, worked as a Professor of Egyptology.

Matilde was the opposite of Camille – she never wore a skirt or carried a handbag and her pockets were always full of penknives, magnifying glasses and strange ancient objects that she had found. She had crazy, curly black hair and little square glasses that always seemed to be slipping down her nose. Matilde had a daughter named Agnes, who looked exactly like a mini version of Matilde, except she had her father's dark skin. He was an Egyptian archaeologist named Akhil and, although Matilde and he were divorced, they were still great friends. Akhil lived around the corner from Matilde, and Agnes went between the two houses. Violet and Agnes were almost exactly the same age and, despite the fact that Violet lived in London and Agnes lived in Cairo, they knew each other very well because they often stayed together with Grand-mère in the south of France.

Agnes and Violet got on brilliantly *most* of the time, but they did have their quarrels, usually because Agnes was what you would describe as a little, or more accurately a lot, on the naughty side. She particularly loved practical jokes. Sometimes they were great fun and Violet was happy to play along, but sometimes Agnes went too far and got them into lots of trouble. For instance, last time they had all stayed at Grand-mère's, Agnes had persuaded Violet to hide Agnes's pet rat, Mr Ratty, in Benedict and Camille's bed. Agnes adored Mr Ratty and Violet could see that he was rather sweet in a furry, brown, ratty sort of way. He lived in a small bag, called the Ratbag, which Agnes carried everywhere. Anyway, for most people, finding a rat in your bed would be bad enough, but Mr Ratty had a particular fondness for people's noses and had bitten Benedict's as Violet's father had tried to remove the rat from the bed. Benedict had ended up with a large plaster on his nose and had failed to see anything funny about the joke.

I could go on, but we need to get back to the postcard. On it, written in Agnes's large, loopy handwriting, were the words, *J'ARRIVE!!!* which means *I'M COMING!!!* in French. Violet was baffled. Her mother hadn't mentioned that her aunt and cousin

were coming to stay, and when she asked Norma she had no idea either. *Oh well,* Violet thought, *I'll ask Mama later.*

Six o'clock was the magical hour for the Remy-Robinsons, when Violet's mother and father, having finished work, would drink a cocktail and discuss their day with Violet. That evening, as her parents sipped hot rum punch, Violet showed them the postcard. Camille was as puzzled as Violet, and was about to say so, when the telephone rang. Benedict picked it up, while Camille and Violet listened.

'Hello? Hello, Matilde, how are you? We were just talking about you . . . You have some exciting news? . . . Shall I pass you to Camille? . . . No, okay . . .' There was a long pause. 'Well, that does sound exciting. Queen Nefertiti? Really? And the mummy is here in the British Museum? . . . So you're coming to London next week . . . and Agnes? She's coming too . . . How . . . er . . . marvellous . . . Here's Camille . . . she's desperate to talk to you . . .'

Camille took the receiver and immediately started gabbling in French to her sister.

'Matilde thinks that there's a link between Queen Nefertiti and a mummy in the British Museum. She's coming over to investigate further. She thinks the mummy may lead to Nefertiti's long-lost tomb!' Benedict explained to Violet.

'Wow! That would be amazing!' Violet gasped. 'It would be as incredible as when Tutankhamun was found.' As far as Violet was concerned, Ancient Egypt was the most interesting thing that she had ever studied at school.

'I agree that is very exciting, but Akhil is away on a dig, so it does mean that Agnes is coming with Matilde,' Benedict said rather unenthusiastically, taking a large slurp of rum punch.

'Oh, it's going to be such fun!' Camille exclaimed, having said goodbye to her sister.

'I'm just saying this now so there's absolutely

no confusion,' Benedict said, stroking his nose protectively. 'I am not having that rat in our flat under any circumstances.'

Camille swung immediately into action and over the next week she had arranged for Matilde and Agnes to rent a teeny flat across the garden, in the building next to Violet's great friends, Dee Dee and Art. And, because they might be spending some time in England, Camille had persuaded Violet's headmistress, Mrs Rumperbottom, to allow Agnes to attend St Catherine's for the rest of the term.

'Are you sure that's a good idea?' Benedict had asked, when he thought Violet wasn't listening. 'Agnes can be quite . . . boisterous.'

'I'm aware of that but Matilde assures me that she is much calmer, and has hardly been in trouble at all recently, so I'm sure it will work out perfectly,' Camille replied with a dismissive wave of her hand.

2
AGNES'S FIRST DAY AT SCHOOL

8.30 a.m.: Mrs Register, the form teacher

'Well, girls, I'd like you all to welcome Violet's cousin, Agnes. She lives in Cairo in Egypt normally, but she's going to spend the rest of the term with us here, which is nice. So I'd like you all to be kind to Agnes while she settles in. It can be very scary starting a new school.'

10.30 a.m.: Mr Comma, the English teacher

'I know it's your first day, Agnes, but I would appreciate it if you would stop talking. And Violet and Rose, stop listening. Thank you.'

10.35 a.m.

'Agnes!'

10.40 a.m.

'I'm sorry to do this on your first day, Agnes, but I am going to have to warn you properly. At St Catherine's, if you talk in class, you get something called a debit. If you say another word, you are going to get one. If you get three debits in a week then you have to go and see the headmistress.'

10.45 a.m.

'I'm sorry, but I am going to give you all – Violet, Rose and Agnes – a debit.'

11 a.m.: Agnes and Violet, breaktime

'I cannot believe, Violet, that you have a best friend who cries when she gets told off.'
'Don't be mean. Rose has just never had a

debit before.'

11.30 a.m.: Miss Sums, the maths teacher

'Is that a note in your hand, Violet? Bring it up here immediately! Well, I can see it's not your writing, but you know we don't pass notes here. I'm giving you a debit for setting such a bad example to your cousin. And whoever wrote this, I'm sorry you felt the need to be rude about the size of my bottom.'

1 p.m.: Rose, lunchtime
'No, really, Violet, you must sit with Agnes – she's your cousin and it's her first day. I'm

quite happy sitting with Lydia.'

2 p.m.: Mr Paint, the art teacher

'Is that a RAT in here? How revolting! Up on your chairs while I try and catch it! How did it get in here? What did you say, Agnes? I see. Kindly get your rat then and, since it's your first day, as long as you don't ever, ever bring it back into school, we won't say anything else about it.'

3.45 p.m.: Violet, Rose and Agnes, on the way home from school

A frosty silence, broken by Agnes.

'So, Violet, can we play in the garden when we get back?'

'I've got a climbing lesson and then a chess lesson, but maybe quickly after that.'

'Would you like to play?' Agnes asked Rose half-heartedly.

'No thank you,' Rose replied briskly. 'I've got my ballet class.'

'Ballet?' Agnes sneered. 'What – do you waltz around in a tutu – all la-la-la? Don't you find that SO boring?'

'No, not at all,' Rose replied coldly.

'You should try kung fu, it's so much more fun!' And Agnes

did a few moves for Rose. 'Did I tell you I'm a black belt? Which is, like, the best. I am a lethal weapon.'

'Yes, I think you did mention it on the way to school, and then at breaktime, and then again at lunchtime,' Rose said.

5.45 p.m.: the communal garden

By coincidence, Violet and Rose wandered

out into the garden at the same moment that evening, having finished their homework and activities. It was practically dark and Art and some other children were finishing a game of football. Both girls saw Agnes tackle Stanley, Rose's older brother, and then kick the ball effortlessly through the goal. Everyone cheered and slapped her on the back.

'She's cool, your cousin,' Art said to Violet, who, like Rose, gave him a small, tight smile.

7 p.m.: supper at the Remy-Robinson house

'Do you all have what you want?' Camille asked, as everyone sprinkled cheese over their pasta. 'Violet, fetch some more water, please. Cheers! Now, I want to hear all about your first days. Agnes, how was school?'

Agnes smiled angelically at Camille. 'It was fun, but nothing much happened; I don't think that the teachers even noticed me. And Rose is so sweet. I *love* how she does ballet the whole time.'

Violet shot Agnes a look, but she ignored it.

'Excellent. I'm glad it went well,' Camille said. 'And how was the museum, Matilde?'

'It was good too, but more eventful,' Matilde replied, and she began to drink, eat her pasta and talk all at the same time. 'I met the famous Archie Fitzherbert.'

'Who's he?' Violet asked.

'He's the new Head of the British Museum. Everyone was amazed when he got the job, as he's only bought and sold artefacts for his rich clients before.'

'What's an artefact?' Violet asked.

Agnes jumped in. 'An artefact is an object, often of archaeological importance.'

'It's a fancy word for thing,' Benedict said. 'Usually an old thing.'

Matilde laughed. 'It's true. Professor Fitzherbert told me how unrewarding he found his old job, and how delighted he was to work in a museum where everyone could visit. Anyway, he was very welcoming and

couldn't have been more charming. In fact, I was having a lovely time until I saw you-know-who.'

Camille laughed.

Benedict and Violet looked mystified so Agnes explained.

'Professor Petit works at the British Museum too and is Mama's great rival. He is obsessed with finding Nefertiti's tomb.'

'We all grew up together,' Camille said. 'I remember Pierre Petit chasing us down the beach near Grand-mère's, swearing he'd get his revenge on you one day after you pushed him in the water.'

'And he never has,' Matilde replied with

satisfaction. 'And now he's furious because he has spent the last twenty years searching for Nefertiti's tomb and he cannot bear the thought that I might find it.'

'Rude as he is, I would like to see him again,' Camille said. 'I think I'll throw a little welcome party for you and Agnes. You can invite some people from the museum and I'll invite some of our friends so you can meet them properly.'

'Thank you, that sounds fun,' Matilde replied.

'Oh, my goodness me!' Benedict exclaimed. 'I nearly forgot to tell you! Look what I saw in the newspaper today.' And he pulled a sheet of newsprint from his pocket and unfolded it, handing it to Violet.

The article was called Celebrity Cop and there was a large photo of Violet's friend, PC Green, grinning at the camera in his uniform.

'He's written a book,' Benedict went on, 'called *Solving Crime: The Green Method*, which is an international bestseller. He's a superstar among police officers apparently.'

Violet's mouth dropped open. Thankfully, it was empty and not full of spaghetti bolognese.

'Well, let's invite him to our party,' Camille said. 'It's always nice to have someone famous.'

The party was arranged for the following Saturday. Norma didn't work at the weekend so Benedict spent the whole day cooking, while Violet and Camille were in charge of drinks and getting the flat ready, which involved a lot of shopping and moving furniture. At last it was done and at six o'clock, when the doorbell rang, the flat looked immaculate, the Remy-Robinsons were dressed in their party clothes and the smell of deliciously yummy food filled the air.

Dee Dee and Art were the first to arrive. Dee Dee looked rather fabulous in a lime-green kaftan and a sort of jewelled headdress. She was clutching a large rubber plant as a present, which she thrust at a surprised Camille. Art was wearing a shirt and trousers, and looking slightly sheepish, as he always did when Dee Dee made him smarten up. Rose and her parents arrived moments later, Stanley was busy playing football which he said was much more fun than a boring old party.

'Welcome, everyone! Let me get you all a drink,' Benedict said. 'I could do with some help, you three.' He turned to Violet, Rose and Art. They looked pleased, because it's always fun to help at parties, isn't it? Benedict handed Rose a tray of drinks and Art a plate of sausage rolls. 'Violet, please can you be in charge of answering the door?' he said.

The doorbell rang again and Violet opened the front door to reveal a very small, very wide man. He had black hair, a neat little beard and he was wearing a pinstriped suit with a waistcoat and a bow tie. He carried an umbrella, although it wasn't raining, and a large packet of dog biscuits.

'Who are you?' he asked Violet in a cross way, as if *she* had rung on his doorbell, not the other way round. He spoke English with a very strong French accent.

'I'm Violet. And you are?'

'Ah yes, Camille's daughter.' He bent down and peered at her. 'You look nothing like her,' he said in the same grumpy way.

'I am Professor Pierre Petit,' he announced grandly.

Violet longed to be rude back to him, but she knew two wrongs don't make a right, so she replied politely.

40

'Please come in. May I take your coat?'

'No, but please will you put my umbrella somewhere VERY SAFE, so no one steals it? These are a present for your dog.' He held out the dog biscuits.

'Er, thank you,' Violet replied. 'Actually, we don't have a dog, but my cockatoo might like them.'

'You don't have a dog? How very peculiar!'

'We have a cat, Pudding,' Violet replied. 'Unfortunately, he hates parties so he's hiding under my bed. Our cockatoo, the Maharani, is in her cage in the sitting room . . .' But Professor Petit wasn't listening as his attention was now firmly on Camille who had just come

into the hallway with Benedict.

'Goodness me, how time passes! I barely recognise you, Camille.'

'Or I you, Pierre,' Camille replied, arching an eyebrow at him. 'But I can see that your personality is just the same. This is my husband, Benedict.'

Brrring!! The doorbell rang again. Violet rushed to open the door, glad to have an excuse to stop talking to the rude professor. Outside were Matilde and Agnes, along with PC Green.

'Oh, have you three met?'

'Yes, just now,' Matilde said, winking at Violet. 'PC Green has told us all about his new-found fame.'

Sure enough, PC Green was carrying a pile of his books with him.

'Hello, Violet, I just brought a few copies along in case anyone wanted a signed one. And some photos too,' he said, whipping out some large copies of the photo of him that Violet had seen in the newspaper.

'Great,' Violet replied, as kindly as she could. 'Come in.'

Is that everyone? Violet wondered, trying to remember the guest list. A few moments later, the bell rang again.

Violet opened the door to a very tall, slim man, with a slight stoop. He had swept-back grey hair, a large nose that he seemed to have to peer over to speak to Violet, and pale blue eyes with heavy lids, like a lizard. He was clutching a bottle of dry sherry.

'Good evening, young lady,' he said smoothly. 'I am Archie Fitzherbert and I was invited to a party here this evening.'

Oh yes, Violet thought. *Matilde's boss at the museum.*

'Of course,' she said. 'Please come in – everyone's through here. I'm Violet, Matilde's niece.'

'Violet, I am delighted to meet you,' he replied.

He seems nice, Violet thought and decided she would introduce him to Dee Dee. Dee Dee, who had been a young actress in 1950s Hollywood, was chatting to PC Green about the problems of fame.

'Everyone wants a piece of me,' PC Green was complaining. 'And I feel under such pressure.'

'Oh, my dear, I do remember. It must be terrible for you,' Dee Dee sympathised in her Southern belle accent.

'Of course, it has been a distraction from breaking up with Maria,' PC Green added with a deep sigh. Maria was PC Green's Italian ex-girlfriend.

'You'll meet someone else, I'm sure,' Dee

Dee said.

'Dee Dee,' Violet said. 'This is Archie Fitzherbert. He is Head of the British Museum.'

'How enchanting to meet you,' Dee exclaimed, offering her hand. 'I am Dee Dee Derota and this is PC Green.'

Art and Rose appeared with more drinks and sausage rolls and everyone was introduced. Dee Dee was about to launch into further chitchat, when Professor Petit appeared, holding out his glass to Rose for more wine and, with his other hand, scooping up sausage rolls which he proceeded to shovel into his mouth.

'Thank goodness you are here! What

a strange collection of people,' he said to Professor Fitzherbert with his mouth still full of food. Then he turned to Dee Dee and PC Green and said, 'Why have you come in fancy dress?'

'We haven't!' PC Green exclaimed. 'I am a real policeman!'

Professor Petit laughed, turning to Dee Dee. 'And I suppose you are a real lime?'

Dee Dee looked confused at first and was just starting to be offended when Professor Fitzherbert stepped in.

'Madam, you look delightful. You mustn't mind Professor Petit – he's not very good at saying the right thing. So, PC Green, you're a

policeman, how interesting. Tell me, what crimes have you solved?'

'Well, apart from a tricky case involving a lost cat, I've mostly worked with Violet, Rose and Art, haven't I?' He turned to the three children, who nodded. 'So together we have solved the case of the smugglers in Italy, the loss of Mrs Derota's brooch, the Pearl of the Orient, and then the kidnapping of the Maharani, Violet's cockatoo.'

'Really?' Professor Fitzherbert said, looking at the three of them 'Are you budding detectives?'

'Less of the budding, more of the expert,'

PC Green said proudly.

'How impressive,' said Professor Fitzherbert. 'We recently had some thefts from the back area of the museum where we all work. Nothing that important, just some minor pieces.'

'I wouldn't say that,' Professor Petit said huffily. 'They are all fine examples of New Kingdom objects – there was that very interesting scarab amulet and a gold ring . . .'

Professor Fitzherbert continued. 'One of your colleagues, Inspector Jones, came to investigate,' he said to PC Green.

'Dolores Jones? Oh, she's brilliant; she does all the top cases,' PC Green said approvingly.

'Yes, she was very helpful, but unfortunately

she couldn't find the thief,' Professor Fitzherbert said.

Violet, Art and Rose, who, as you know, loved solving crimes, were positively twitching with questions for the Professor about the thefts, but at that moment Matilde strode over with Agnes.

'Ah, I'm so pleased you've already met the other children,' she said, greeting Professor Fitzherbert. 'This is my daughter,' she said, gesturing to Agnes.

Matilde wished Professor Petit a good evening, but he was too busy shoving yet another sausage roll in his mouth to do more than give her and Agnes a curt nod.

Turning back to Professor Fitzherbert, Matilde said, 'Would it be all right if I brought the children into the museum at half-term to have a look around and see the mummy I'm working on? It's in two weeks' time.'

Professor Petit made a sort of spluttering sound, but Professor Fitzherbert replied, 'Of course, that would be fine.'

'Do you think we could ask some questions too about the thefts? Just to see if we could get any further than the police?' Violet asked.

'Yes, be my guest,' Professor Fitzherbert replied with a smile. 'Now, let me taste one of these delicious-looking sausage rolls before Pierre eats them all.'

'I have to admit they are very good,' Professor Petit said, taking three more.

I am sad to report that despite Agnes having been told that under no circumstances was Mr Ratty to come to the party, he had somehow ended up in her pocket and the tantalising smell of all those sausage rolls was proving too much for him. He poked his head out to have a look at just the moment Professor Petit was sneaking a sausage roll into the pocket of his suit. The temptation was overwhelming for Mr Ratty and he launched himself at the Professor.

Well, you can just imagine the kerfuffle that followed. Professor Petit started shrieking that

he was being attacked by a rodent, Matilde was shouting at Agnes and Agnes was shouting at Mr Ratty, who had scuttled under a chest of drawers with a large hunk of sausage roll. The Maharani began to squawk and Benedict had an expression like a thundercloud, while Rose, Art and Violet got the terrible giggles. And PC Green, Dee Dee and Professor Fitzherbert all politely excused themselves and thanked Camille for a lovely party.

4
AN AMAZING DISCOVERY

Violet decided that they should speak to Inspector Jones before their half-term visit so she made an appointment for them all to meet her at the police station. Dee Dee offered to take them, as her cat, Lullabelle, needed her toenails clipping, and the vet was nearby.

Inspector Jones, or Dolores as she insisted they call her, was a very nice, sensible young woman and they all liked her immediately. She knew all about the other cases that they had solved and, unlike most grown-ups, she treated them like proper detectives. Over tea and biscuits, she talked them through her record of the thefts at the museum. Rose took some notes and they looked like this.

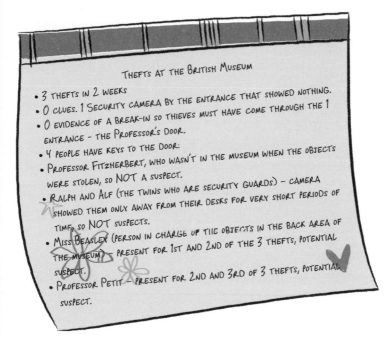

THEFTS AT THE BRITISH MUSEUM

- 3 THEFTS IN 2 WEEKS
- 0 CLUES. 1 SECURITY CAMERA BY THE ENTRANCE THAT SHOWED NOTHING.
- 0 EVIDENCE OF A BREAK-IN SO THIEVES MUST HAVE COME THROUGH THE 1 ENTRANCE - THE PROFESSOR'S DOOR.
- 4 PEOPLE HAVE KEYS TO THE DOOR:
- PROFESSOR FITZHERBERT, WHO WASN'T IN THE MUSEUM WHEN THE OBJECTS WERE STOLEN, SO NOT A SUSPECT.
- RALPH AND ALF (THE TWINS WHO ARE SECURITY GUARDS) - CAMERA SHOWED THEM ONLY AWAY FROM THEIR DESKS FOR VERY SHORT PERIODS OF TIME, SO NOT SUSPECTS.
- MISS BEASLEY (PERSON IN CHARGE OF THE OBJECTS IN THE BACK AREA OF THE MUSEUM) - PRESENT FOR 1ST AND 2ND OF THE 3 THEFTS, POTENTIAL SUSPECT.
- PROFESSOR PETIT - PRESENT FOR 2ND AND 3RD OF 3 THEFTS, POTENTIAL SUSPECT.

'Could Professor Petit and Miss Beasley have been working together?' Art asked.

Dolores nodded. 'I definitely thought that there was more than one thief, and I did wonder whether those two were working jointly. What was strange was that they denied being friends, but then one of the guards from the main museum said that they always had lunch together. However, I couldn't find any real evidence, which as you know is what you need. So I had no choice but to close the case. Hopefully, you'll have more luck!'

I don't know if you have ever been to the British Museum in London, but it is so

ENORMOUS that, when you go in, beneath its great grey entrance, you feel like an ant walking under an elephant. Matilde led Rose, Art, Violet and Agnes briskly up the steps, and through the half-term crowds towards the Professor's door at the back of the museum.

Unfortunately, Rose and Agnes were not getting on any better, which was frustrating for Violet as she felt that neither of them was giving the other a proper chance. So Violet had spent some time persuading Agnes to let Rose come to the museum and telling Rose that Agnes really wanted her to be there. In the end, Rose's desire to see the mummy and

to find out more about the thefts had won her over.

Matilde was humming a jolly tune as they reached a large door that said

STAFF ONLY

In front of it sat a scrawny young man dressed in a guard's uniform.

'Good morning, Alf,' Matilde said, grinning at him.

'Good morning, Professor. You seem in a very good mood,' he replied.

'I am,' Matilde said. 'This is my daughter, Agnes, my niece, Violet, and her friends, Art and Rose. All of you, this is Alf. He and his identical twin brother, Ralph, have both just finished studying Egyptology at university and are working here as guards while they're waiting for a chance to go on an archaeological dig in Egypt.'

The children said hello politely to Alf, who was looking at them with amusement.

'You must be the young detectives I've heard about?' When they nodded, he said, 'Well, perhaps you can solve the mystery of our thefts. Feel free to ask me any questions.'

Rose got out a pen and notebook and they checked the information about the Professor's door and the camera that Dolores had given them. Alf confirmed it was all correct.

'I have just have one more question,' Violet

said. 'Was it you or your brother who was working when the objects were stolen?'

'It was Ralph the first two times, and me the last time,' Alf said. 'But surely you don't suspect me?' he joked. 'I can assure you I am entirely innocent. Here, let me bribe you with a mint humbug.' He produced a bag from under his desk.

The children smiled and, thanking him, took a sweet.

'Well, if those are all the questions,' Matilde said. 'Follow me. I want to introduce you to my mummy, Tey.'

In the corridor, a lady walked past them, carrying a small statue as carefully as if it was a newborn baby.

'Girls, this is Miss Beasley, our cataloguer. She is an expert on all things Egyptian, but particularly New Kingdom artefacts,' Matilde said. 'The New Kingdom was the time in Ancient Egypt when Tutankhamun and Nefertiti lived,' she added.

Miss Beasley was very slim, with streaky grey hair pulled back tightly into a bun, and spiky-looking glasses. She didn't seem particularly friendly, though she did manage to say hello, and that she hoped that they'd have an interesting time, BUT please could they not touch ANYTHING they weren't supposed to.

Tey, the mummy, was laid out on a table in a small white room that looked a little like a laboratory.

'Oh, isn't she a perfect example of a New Kingdom mummy? But perhaps not as good as the one my father excavated . . .' Agnes burbled on, while the others stood silently, fascinated by the grave-faced, golden-masked figure.

'How old is she?' Rose asked Matilde.

'Over three thousand years old,' Matilde replied.

Rose gasped.

Agnes rolled her eyes. 'That's not very old

for a mummy,' she said meanly.

Violet felt like pinching Agnes, while Matilde tutted at her daughter and turned to Rose.

'Ignore her, Rose. I'm afraid Agnes has become too used to being around ancient artefacts. Three thousand years is very old for anything. Now, let me explain to you all a little about what I've been doing. I have actually been studying the mummy case and the coffin, rather than the mummy itself, and also the objects she was buried with, as these give greater clues to her identity. Come and look – they're over here.'

The case and coffin were made of wood and

painted with intricate designs of hieroglyphs and pictures. And then carefully laid on a table were an assortment of large jars, little statuettes and some jewellery. Violet was in heaven.

'Those are Canopic jars, aren't they?' she said excitedly. When Matilde nodded, she went on. 'We learnt about those in our school project – they have the mummy's liver and heart in them, don't they?'

'Yes, and look at these little amulets,' Matilde said. 'They are charms that were buried with mummies, for good luck. And these are shabtis,' she explained, picking up one of the figures. 'They were slaves for the mummy in

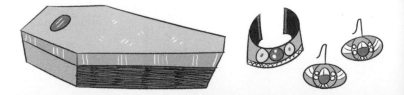

the afterlife . . .'

'You wanted to see me?' A voice interrupted Matilde and they all turned around to see Professor Fitzherbert standing in the doorway.

Matilde's face lit up. 'Yes, I wanted to show you what I have just uncovered. It's a set of hieroglyphs identifying this lady as Nefertiti's beloved nurse, Tey, as I thought.'

'Really! That is fascinating!' he exclaimed and the two of them went to huddle over the coffin.

'And what's even more exciting is that I've started translating the next section, and I think it will confirm that Tey was buried near Nefertiti,' Matilde said. 'I am very hopeful

that I'll be able to work out the exact location of Nefertiti's tomb in the Valley of the Kings. It would make perfect sense for Nefertiti – as a queen – to have been buried there.'

Professor Fitzherbert swallowed hard and took a deep breath. 'That indeed would be remarkable. The lost tomb of Nefertiti. Imagine the treasures . . .'

'Are we running a nursery now?' a voice interrupted them. Professor Petit strode into the room. 'Matilde, I do hope you are not letting these children touch anything.'

The four friends exchanged glances.

'Of course not,' Matilde replied.

'Matilde has made the most remarkable

discovery,' Professor Fitzherbert said, his voice quivering with excitement.

'Oh really?' Professor Petit asked, his eyes narrowing with irritation.

'Yes,' Matilde said happily. 'As I thought, this mummy is Tey, and I expect that she will lead me to Nefertiti's tomb.'

Professor Petit's face turned a purply-red.

'No! You cannot have found out such a thing. You are wrong! I have spent my whole life looking for Nefertiti's tomb. No! It cannot be!!' And he stormed out.

They all loved their visit to the museum, and were fascinated by the mummy. But, when the four of them talked about their visit later, they agreed that it hadn't helped them make much progress with solving the crimes. Rose had noticed another piece of evidence pointing towards Miss Beasley – that she was an expert on the New Kingdom and all the items stolen were from that period of history. But then,

CRIME TO SOLVE: THEFT OF ARTEFACTS FROM BRITISH MUSEUM

WERE THERE ANY WITNESSES TO THE CRIME?
NO

WHAT CLUES WERE THERE?
NONE

WHAT CONCLUSIONS CAN BE DRAWN FROM THIS?
NONE!!

as Agnes said rather unkindly, so were her mother, her father, Professor Fitzherbert and Professor Petit, so it was hardly conclusive evidence.

To try and help, they turned Rose's notes into a crime-solving matrix.

ARE THERE ANY SUSPECTS?
PROFESSOR PETIT, MISS BEASLEY

DO THEY HAVE A MOTIVE?
PROFESSOR PETIT HAS THE STRONGEST

DU THEY HAVE AN ALIBI?
PROFESSOR PETIT AND MISS BEASLEY EACH
HAVE AN ALIBI FOR ONE OF THE CRIMES

DOES THIS LEAD YOU TO A
SENSIBLE CONCLUSION?
PROFESSOR PETIT AND MISS BEASLEY APPEAR
THE MOST LIKELY CULPRITS, WORKING TOGETHER

Disappointingly, it didn't tell them much more than they knew from talking to Inspector Jones. Violet hated an unsolved case, but she knew that there was nothing to be done unless there was another theft, so they just had to hope that if the criminals did strike again, they left some more clues.

SQUAWK!

HISS!!

As it turned out, Violet didn't have to wait
very long for another theft. It was early
on the Friday morning after half-term, the
Maharani and Pudding were having a noisy
squabble and Violet was just pouring a twirl
of golden syrup onto her porridge when the
telephone rang. Shortly after, her mother
came into the kitchen in a fluster.

'That was poor Matilde in a terrible state!
Her mummy has been stolen.'

'Someone has stolen Grand-mère?' Benedict teased, waving his piece of toast and marmalade around in the air. 'Good Lord. I bet that was quite a business.'

Camille shot him a look. 'Her mummy at the museum.'

'But that's terrible. When did it happen?' Violet asked. She hadn't ever imagined something as important as the mummy being stolen.

'Last night at some point. Professor Fitzherbert came into the museum very early and raised the alarm. Apparently, Inspector Jones is busy on another case so Professor Fitzherbert requested that PC Green come and investigate.'

'Oh dear,' Benedict replied.

Agnes and Rose still weren't getting on, but the mummy theft gave them something to focus on, and they agreed with Violet that they couldn't leave PC Green to solve the case on his own.

'Why don't you all come over to my flat after school?' Violet said in the playground at breaktime. 'We could get Art to come too and then we can telephone PC Green and see what he's found out.'

'Good plan,' Rose said. 'I'll fetch Art when we get back.'

'No, I will – I live next door to him,'

Agnes said.

'But I can just as easily get him,' Rose said, frowning.

'We can all go and pick him up,' Violet snapped, feeling thoroughly irritated with both of them.

But, when they got home from school, Norma said, 'You have a visitor,' and sure enough, there in the kitchen sat none other than PC Green, munching through a pile of Norma's freshly baked chocolate-chip cookies.

'Hi, chaps! Gosh, am I pleased to see you! This mummy case is really tricky. I am COMPLETELY stumped. And there is SO much media pressure. I could really use your help, if you don't mind.'

'We'd like that, wouldn't we?' Violet said to the others, who nodded. 'I'll just get Art,' Violet said, and sprinted off before Rose or Agnes could object. 'Don't eat all the biscuits,' she called over her shoulder. She returned with Art a few moments later.

'PC Green, why don't you tell us all the facts, and Rose, do you want to get out the crime-solving matrix so we can add to it?' Violet said. 'All we really established before was that the thefts must have been committed by two people working together and the most likely pair was Miss Beasley and Professor Petit,' she explained to the policeman.

PC Green gave a thoughtful sigh and pulled out his notebook, as the others sat round the table.

'So, chaps, according to Professor Fitzherbert, when he arrived at the museum at seven this morning, the mummy was gone. There were no obvious signs of a break-in and the security guard, Ralph, said that he had seen nothing unusual when he did his rounds during the night. There had been no deliveries or visitors and the Professor's door was locked.'

'Was it just the mummy that was stolen or the case and the coffin too?' Rose asked.

'All of it,' PC Green confirmed.

'Did the security camera show anything?'

Violet asked

'No, it was disconnected by the thief.'

Everyone tutted with irritation.

'However,' PC Green went on, 'between about five in the morning and six, no one was at the museum – Ralph had finished his shift and Alf was late arriving because their mother is ill. Poor lads, their father died recently too. So for an hour no one was there.'

'It must have happened then,' Agnes said. 'Did anyone see the mummy after that?'

'Gosh, you're on the ball,' PC Green said. 'No, I don't think so. But Alf did say that everything seemed fine when he arrived and the doors were locked, as they should be.'

'That would suggest that whoever took the mummy had a key,' Rose said.

PC Green nodded. 'Yes. Pity I forgot to ask who has keys.'

'It's all right, Dolores told us,' Rose said, looking at her notes. 'Ralph and Alf, Professor Fitzherbert, Miss Beasley and Professor Petit all have keys.'

'Hmm, interesting. I talked to each of them about what they got up to last night. Let me tell you what they said.' He did a lot of flicking through the pages in his notebook.

'Professor Fitzherbert left the museum at six-thirty to go and visit his elderly father –

isn't that nice? He was seen by Miss Beasley and Ralph. Then Miss Beasley left at six forty-five and she spent the evening at home with her sister. She was seen by Ralph.'

'And Professor Petit?'

PC Green let out a little snort. 'He's a very rude man. He called me an idiot and refused to answer any of my questions until Professor Fitzherbert stepped in and told him he had to. Apparently, he left at nine-thirty, but no one saw him,' PC Green said. Three pairs of eyebrows shot up at PC Green as if to say, *There you go then.* 'But Ralph did mention that he was patrolling at that time so might not have seen him.'

'Now, what about motives?' Art said. 'Do you think the mummy has been stolen to find the location of Nefertiti's tomb?'

'Well, not necessarily,' PC Green replied, going back to his notebook. 'Professor Fitzherbert said a mummy like that is incredibly valuable and that it could just be a coincidence.'

'That's true,' Agnes said. 'The mummy is probably worth millions.'

'I think it seems too much of a coincidence,' Violet said.

'When we were at the museum, Professor Petit got very angry about Matilde possibly having discovered the location of Nefertiti's tomb,' Art said. 'Do you think he might want to sabotage her research?'

'He's always been jealous of Mama,' Agnes said.

'But he might want Nefertiti's tomb to be found, even if it was by someone else,' Rose pointed out.

'Dolores was suspicious that Professor Petit and Miss Beasley were involved in the previous thefts,' Violet said. 'And we do know that Miss Beasley is particularly keen on New Kingdom artefacts.'

'So they both have a motive,' PC Green said. 'But they both left the museum before five in the morning.'

'They could have come back,' Violet said.

'We shouldn't just rule out everyone else without examining the facts first,' Rose said, the sensible one as always.

'The only other people with keys are Ralph and Alf and Professor Fitzherbert. And I shouldn't think Professor Fitzherbert would steal from his own museum,' Violet said.

'It's not exactly his museum,' Rose pointed out. 'But he does run it and if Matilde uncovered Nefertiti's tomb it would make the museum even more famous.'

'He used to sell artefacts to people, didn't he?' Art asked Agnes.

'Yes,' she replied. 'But he told Mama that

he didn't enjoy it and wanted to work in a museum where everyone can see the objects.'

'Well, that's very nice of him,' PC Green said.

'What about Ralph and Alf?' Violet asked.

'I did wonder about them, so I had a quick word with Professor Fitzherbert. He said that they are incredibly trustworthy and reliable and had worked for him before. They were part of the new team he brought in when he started,' PC Green said.

'Along with Miss Beasley,' Agnes said.

'It does all seem to point to Professor Petit and Miss Beasley,' Rose said, showing them the updated crime-solving matrix.

'You guys are amazing,' PC Green said with a sigh of relief. 'It's so much clearer now. So, where do you think they would hide this mummy?'

'We should start by searching their homes,' Rose said.

'Good idea. Look, I've got their addresses here.' More flicking through pages. 'Professor Petit lives at 14 Elmbridge Villas, and Miss Beasley lives at the Basement Flat, 35 Arcadia Road. I'll get back to the station and fill out the forms for search warrants. It's so speedy now – I should have them in about a week.'

'A week!' Agnes spluttered. 'They could have moved the mummy anywhere by then!

Can't you do it any quicker?'

'Young lady,' PC Green said gravely, 'you have to respect the process. Right, I'd better be off; there's a press conference later so now I can tell them we have a definite lead, mentioning no names of course. Perhaps I'll just drop a hint that one of them is rude and French . . .'

'No, don't!' Violet said. 'That will alert him!'

'You're right.' PC Green nodded. 'I can't tell you how much I love our teamwork – together we're better! I'll just take another biscuit for the road.'

After he had gone, Agnes asked, 'Is he always so hopeless?'

Rose nodded.

'Yes,' said Violet. 'That's why we have to go and search Miss Beasley's and Professor Petit's homes ourselves. They're both quite near. We can easily go tomorrow morning; we'll just tell our parents that we're going to the sweetshop.' And they all agreed this was an excellent plan, especially if they could find some time to actually buy some sweets on the way home.

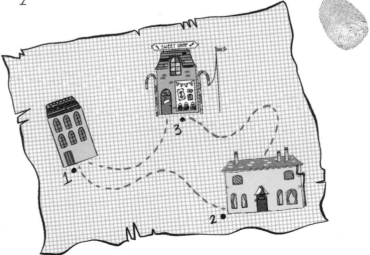

6
NEEDS MUST

The following morning, Rose, Art, Violet and Agnes decided to split up. Rose and Violet would tackle Professor Petit's house, while Art and Agnes would try to get inside Miss Beasley's flat.

Violet and Rose made their plan as they walked to Elmbridge Villas. First, they waited until they saw Professor Petit leave, which, luckily for them, was quite soon after they arrived. And then they walked up to the front

door and Rose nervously rang the doorbell.

Professor Petit's landlady, Mrs Frobisher, opened the door. She was a small, timid woman who loved cats. In fact, when she greeted them, she was holding a large ginger cat in her arms.

'Good morning,' Violet said, speaking English in her best, thick French accent, sounding rather like Grand-mère. 'I am Professor Petit's niece, Marie, and this is my sister, Rose. Is my uncle in?'

'No, I'm afraid he's not. You've just missed

him,' Mrs Frobisher replied.

The girls pretended to look surprised.

'He is expecting us,' Violet said. 'Could we wait for him in his room?'

Mrs Frobisher looked flustered.

'I'm not sure . . . He's a very private man and never lets anyone in his room – not even me. Why don't you wait in the hall?'

Rose thought fast. She did a huge pretend sneeze.

'Unfortunately, I am terribly allergic to cats,' she said in an equally thick French accent. 'I'm sure our uncle wouldn't mind us waiting in his room, as we are family,' she said.

But Mrs Frobisher still wasn't sure. She

was rather terrified of the bad-tempered little Frenchman. Violet could see her wavering, so stepped in.

'Can we just wait for ten minutes? And then if he's not back we'll go away,' she said.

Mrs Frobisher agreed and Violet and Rose exchanged sly grins as she showed them up to the Professor's room. She left them alone as soon as she had unlocked the door, muttering something about having to look after one of her cats.

Professor Petit had two rooms on the first floor of the house, which he used as a bedroom and a sitting room. Violet and Rose half expected to see the mummy laid out before them when they opened the door. But it wasn't. There was just an unmade bed and a mess of clothes, books and dirty dishes. Violet glanced out of the grubby window to see Professor Petit crossing the road, coming back to the house.

'Oh no,' she gasped. 'He's coming back! We need to get out of here. Quick!' She grabbed Rose's hand and ran through the door and down the stairs, colliding with Mrs Frobisher, who was just coming to check on them.

Unfortunately, at that very moment, the front door opened, revealing Professor Petit.

'What are you two doing here?' he demanded.

'That's not a very nice way to greet your nieces!' Mrs Frobisher said. 'Especially when they've come all the way from France to see you.'

Professor Petit looked confused. 'They are not my nieces and they most certainly haven't come from France – these *little girls* live around the corner.'

There was a silence.

'I can explain,' Violet said, although her mind was empty. She felt like someone jumping off a cliff, hoping that a parachute would appear from thin air and save her. Rose's brain was a terrified blank too. They were going to be in so much trouble.

'Please do,' Professor Petit said coldly.

'Yes, please do,' echoed Mrs Frobisher. 'I am so sorry, Professor. I would never have let them into your rooms if I'd known.'

'You have been in my rooms!' he cried, furious. 'You had no right, no right at all!'

'I'm sorry. We just wanted to ask you some questions about the disappearance of the mummy,' Violet said.

'Oh really?' he asked sarcastically. 'Well, why didn't you wait until I came back then? I suppose you think *I* took the mummy?'

Violet and Rose went a bit red and looked at their feet.

'Right, come on, we'll see what your mother has to say about this, Violet.'

As you might have expected, Camille was not amused. She told Professor Petit how very sorry she was and made the girls apologise repeatedly. When he had gone, she said, 'Rose, I think you had better go home. I want to speak to Violet on her own.'

Rose nodded and scampered off to find Art and Agnes.

'Violet, I'm very disappointed in you. Professor Petit may be bad-tempered, but he is not a bad man; he would not have stolen the mummy. And, even if you did suspect him, you cannot just search people's houses without their permission. You should leave the investigating to PC Green.'

'But it was going to take him a week to get a search warrant, by which time the mummy could have been moved anywhere,' Violet objected. She was itching to go and find out how Art and Agnes had got on.

'Please may I go and play in the garden?' she asked.

'Only after you have tidied your bedroom, done your homework and cleared out the Maharani's cage,' Camille replied calmly.

Violet whirled around her bedroom, furiously tidying, and then sat down and rattled through her homework as quickly as she could. The last job was the worst, for although the Maharani's cage had been specially designed by Benedict, and was very beautiful, cleaning it was still a pretty unpleasant experience. Especially as the Maharani insisted on perching on Violet's shoulder while she did it, squawking 'BAD VIOLET!' into her ear.

Eventually, it was done and Violet dashed out into the garden to find Art and Agnes sitting on a bench with Rose.

'Did you manage to see inside Miss Beasley's flat?'

97

she asked expectantly.

'No, but she was out and as it's a basement flat we looked through the front window. Then Art managed to climb over the gate to the back garden and look through the windows on that side.'

'Until one of the neighbours chased us away,' Art added.

'And?' Violet asked.

'Well, it was quite strange,' Art said. 'Either Miss Beasley is incredibly tidy or she doesn't actually live there. Anyway, there was no sign of the mummy.'

Violet sighed with disappointment. She had been sure that they would find it at one of the houses.

'So what should we do now?' Agnes asked Violet.

'I don't know,' she replied truthfully.

Despite many discussions, and much poring over the crime-solving matrix, the friends were completely stumped and pretty fed up about it.

PC Green didn't fare any better. He interviewed Professor Petit and Miss Beasley again, but they both absolutely denied taking the mummy. Mrs Frobisher even made a statement saying that Professor Petit had arrived home that night at ten, just as she was going to sleep, and could not have left again without her hearing. He went out as normal at eight o'clock the following morning. Miss Beasley's sister had come forward to say that Miss Beasley had spent the night at her sister's flat, and confirming that she too had not left until the following morning.

Since the mummy was so valuable, Interpol, who are the international crime solvers, became involved, but they could find no trace of it either. Finally, all the grown-ups said that the best hope of discovering the mummy was if it turned up for sale to a collector.

Weeks passed and eventually the school term finished. The mummy was still missing and so Matilde had no reason to stay in London. She and Agnes were going home to Cairo at the end of the week.

'How was your last day at the museum?' Benedict asked Matilde, as they sat down for supper.

'They gave me a nice card and a cake, but it was sad because of the robbery,' Matilde replied. 'It would have been such an amazing discovery and I was so close. Anyway, there is some good news: Ralph and Alf have been offered great jobs working on a dig in South America, looking at some amazing Inca remains.'

'I thought they were Egyptologists?' Agnes said, puzzled.

'I know. I was a little surprised too, but apparently a friend of Miss Beasley's arranged it for them. And Professor Petit is away for two weeks, lecturing in Switzerland, and Professor Fitzherbert is coming to Egypt, for three weeks' holiday. We've arranged to meet up – he's keen to see you too, Agnes.'

'So Miss Beasley will be all alone?' Violet asked suspiciously.

'Yes, with whoever they get as the new security guards,' Matilde replied.

'Come on, Violet, you have no real proof that she or Professor Petit were involved in the thefts,' Benedict said.

Violet sighed and said, 'It's just so annoying

not to have found out who stole the mummy.'

'I agree,' Matilde said. 'But I haven't given up hope yet that she'll turn up. And, in the meantime, I have just had an idea that might cheer you up, Violet.' Matilde turned to Camille and Benedict. 'Why doesn't Violet come to Cairo with us?' she asked. 'Just for a week. I spoke to Grand-mère today. She was complaining that she's bored in France and wants to come and visit us. She'll look after Agnes for me, as I'll have so much work to catch up on. It would be so nice for Agnes to have Violet with her and Grand-mère would love it too.'

Benedict and Camille exchanged glances.

'I think that sounds like an excellent idea,' Benedict replied. 'Violet, what do you think?'

Violet hesitated. She would love to go to Egypt, but how would she ever solve the case from there?

Camille read Violet's mind and said, *'Chérie,* a break from thinking about this stolen mummy will do you good. Nothing is likely to change in a week. And think of the fun you will have with Grand-mère and Agnes and all the amazing things you'll see – the pyramids, the Valley of the Kings . . .'

Violet knew her mother was right. She thanked Matilde and said she would love to go. So the plan was made. Art and Rose were very jealous of Violet's visit to Egypt, but in a nice way, and PC Green promised to get in touch if there were any further developments on the case.

7

A Lost Letter

A week later, Violet, Agnes and Grand-mère were standing in the middle of the largest souk in Cairo, which is called the Khan el-Khalili. Now, I need to explain what a souk is – it is an indoor market that you find in Arabic countries. Here there were lots of small stalls and shops selling everything you can imagine, from perfume to chandeliers to slippers to showerheads. Grand-mère was in her absolute element because, if there was one

thing that Grand-mère adored, it was shopping, and shopping where she could have a good old haggle about the price was her idea of heaven. So far she had bought five pink lampshades, three pairs of leather slippers with bells on, a chess set, two backgammon sets, several glass bottles of bath oil and a hookah, which reminded Violet of the caterpillar in *Alice in Wonderland*. And Grand-mère was still going strong. Normally, Violet would have been excruciatingly bored, but it was all so different – the noise, the people, the smells – that she was having a great time.

It was the middle of Violet's week in Egypt – she had been there for three days and had

three days left. They had been to the pyramids and to the Museum of Egyptian Antiquities and they had spent a day sightseeing in Cairo with Agnes's father, Akhil. And that evening, after tea with Professor Fitzherbert, they were to take the overnight train to Luxor to visit the Valley of the Kings, where Tutankhamun and many of the other pharaohs were buried. Violet had loved it all so much that she had almost succeeded in forgetting about the lost mummy.

'Aha!' said Grand-mère with the satisfaction of a hunter who has spotted its prey. 'A tailor. Now *that* is what I really need. I'm feeling so guilty for leaving Alphonse that I must order

him some new little outfits.' Alphonse was Grand-mère's incredibly spoilt French bulldog who had stayed at home in the south of France with a pet sitter.

Agnes knew how long this might take and she wanted to show Violet a shop full of skulls and other spooky, fake Ancient Egyptian artefacts nearby, so she asked Grand-mère if they could go off on their own.

'Very well,' Grand-mère agreed. 'But only for ten minutes and you must be careful. Meet me back here. I will be very cross if you are late,' she said, waving her walking stick for emphasis.

Violet and Agnes were weaving their way down a narrow passage near the tailor's shop when a young European man pushed past them. He looked very familiar to Violet, but she couldn't quite place him. And then she realised in a flash that it was Alf.

'Hello,' she greeted him in a friendly voice. He looked at her blankly and walked briskly on.

'Am I going mad?' Violet asked Agnes. 'Wasn't that Alf?'

'It looked just like him, but he didn't seem to remember us at all,' Agnes replied.

'I know!' cried Violet. 'It must have been Ralph. He's never met us so he wouldn't recognise us.'

'Of course,' Agnes agreed. 'But what's he doing here?'

Violet was puzzled too. 'Wasn't he supposed to be on a dig in South America with his brother?' she said.

'Come on, let's follow him and find out,' Agnes said, grabbing Violet's hand and dragging her in the direction that Ralph had been walking. Unfortunately, they soon lost him in the crowds and they were about to give up when they glimpsed him coming out of a shop.

'There he is!' Agnes said.

But when they reached the spot he was gone. They were by the entrance to the souk and they looked out into the square beyond.

'I can't see him,' Violet said, irritated.

At that moment, the shopkeeper came out of his shop, a letter in his hand.

Agnes began to speak to him in Arabic. Because she had grown up in Cairo, clever Agnes could speak Arabic fluently, as well as French and English.

'Do you know the young man who just left here?' he answered Agnes in English.

'Oh yes, he's our cousin. We're on holiday

with him,' Agnes lied swiftly.

'That is so fortunate. Please will you give him this letter? He must have dropped it in the shop by mistake.'

The girls looked at the envelope. It was just addressed to 'Dad'. *That's strange,* Violet thought. *They told PC Green their father was dead.*

'Oh yes, of course, the letter must be for my uncle,' she replied.

'I thought their father was dead?' Agnes said, as they hurried back to Grand-mère.

'I know,' Violet said. 'It's all very suspicious.' And she slipped the letter into her pocket.

'I think we should have a look at the letter, just in case it's anything to do with the mummy theft,' Violet whispered to Agnes when they got home.

'I agree,' Agnes said. 'It's very strange that Ralph is here.'

'Art taught me a trick to open an envelope without tearing the paper,' Violet said. 'Grand-mère, would you like a cup of coffee?'

'Thank you, darling. I must say I am exhausted after all that shopping.'

'Sit down in the living room and we'll bring it to you,' Violet said, beckoning to Agnes as she went into the kitchen and put the kettle on. Steam started pouring out of its spout, and

Violet held the envelope over it for a minute or so. Then she carefully peeled it open and pulled the letter out.

'That's so cool,' Agnes said, impressed. 'What does it say?'

DEAR DAD,

WELCOME TO CAIRO! I HAVE JUST RETURNED TO THE CITY TO PICK UP SOME MORE EQUIPMENT. THE EXCAVATION IS GOING BRILLIANTLY AND I WILL MEET YOU THERE TOMORROW AS PLANNED. ALF HOPES THAT WE WILL BE ABLE TO BREAK THROUGH VERY SOON –

TO THE WORLD!

LOVE, RALPH

'*Dear Dad?!*' Violet repeated.

'I wonder what they're excavating?' Agnes said.

Both girls paused and looked at each other.

'Do you think it was them all along?' Violet said. 'Maybe they stole the mummy, translated the hieroglyphs and have found the whereabouts of Nefertiti.'

'Well, it is possible,' Agnes said cautiously. 'But it's more likely that they're excavating something else.'

'Or helping someone else,' Violet said thoughtfully. 'It's very strange. Maybe Professor Fitzherbert will know what's going on.'

'Mama has a dictionary of hieroglyphs in her study,' Agnes said. 'We could try and translate the ones in the letter in case they're a clue.'

'Girls, is my coffee ready?' Grand-mère called from the living room. 'And don't forget you need to pack for our trip to the Valley of the Kings. We have to leave for tea with Professor Fitzherbert at Hotel Cairo in an hour and we'll go straight on from there to the station.' She paused before adding, 'Oh, and Agnes, make sure that Mr Ratty is safely in the Ratbag and cannot escape. I do not want him gallivanting around Professor Fitzherbert's hotel.'

'Yes, of course,' Agnes replied.

'Your coffee will just be a moment, Grand-mère,' Violet said, before turning to Agnes. 'You go and get started in the study.'

Violet joined Agnes in Matilde's study. She was poring over the dictionary.

'I think that those first symbols might mean welcome, but then I am struggling a bit. You see those five balls with crosses on the top? They mean beauty. But I'm not sure about the others.'

'Well done,' Violet said. 'That's great start.'

But it soon turned out that translating hieroglyphs wasn't very easy and half an hour later, when Grand-mère once more hurried them to pack their cases, the girls had barely got any further.

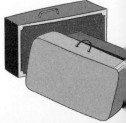

Professor Fitzherbert was sitting at a table in the Hotel Cairo's beautiful terraced gardens, surrounded by a magnificent tea.

'Hello, girls, how lovely to see you!' he said. 'And you must be Madame Remy!'

'It's nice to meet you,' Grand-mère said, shaking his hand. 'I'm sorry Matilde was too busy at work to come.'

'Don't worry. I quite understand,' Professor Fitzherbert replied. 'Now, please, all of you, come and sit down.'

There was a lot of pouring of tea and passing of plates and cake and scones and all sorts of deliciousness, until everyone had what they wanted. Finally, Violet wasn't able to contain herself any longer.

'The strangest thing happened this morning. We saw Ralph in the souk,' she said.

'Ralph from the museum?' Professor Fitzherbert asked, looking surprised.

The girls nodded.

'How extraordinary!' exclaimed the Professor. 'I wonder what he's doing here?'

'Apparently, excavating something with Alf and their father,' Violet replied, and handed Professor Fitzherbert the letter. 'I thought their father was dead.'

'So did I,' he said, reading the letter. 'But I'm sure that there's a perfectly reasonable explanation.'

'Could Professor Petit be their father?' Violet asked. 'Perhaps he lied and he's not lecturing in Switzerland at all, but here excavating something.'

'Gosh, you are the little detective, Violet, aren't you?' Professor Fitzherbert said. 'It's most likely that they got a last-minute job on one of the excavations near the pyramids. Maybe "Dad" is a nickname for someone? Anyway, I don't think that you should spoil your holiday worrying about it any more.

Now, help yourselves to some more of this enormous tea.' And he folded the letter and put it in his pocket.

'Oh, may I have the letter back, please?' Agnes said. 'I'm still trying to translate the hieroglyphics in it.'

'I shouldn't bother if I were you. Come now, have one of these delicious cakes,' he said, offering her a plate of chocolate eclairs.

He doesn't want us to have the letter, Violet thought to herself. *I wonder why?*

'No, really, please may we have the letter back?' she said, looking carefully at the Professor.

He hesitated and Violet saw a flash of

annoyance pass over his face.

'Of course,' he said, and handed it back to Agnes. 'Now, I don't wish to hurry you, but shouldn't you be leaving to catch your train?'

8
Mr Ratty's Return and the Racing Donkey

The train from Cairo to Luxor was an old-fashioned steam train and Grand-mère was in heaven.

'Just like when I was a girl,' she sighed, as the guard showed them to their compartment.

'Dinner will be served in the restaurant car at seven, madam. I do hope you have a comfortable journey.'

Later, when the train had chugged out of the station and the sun was setting in the rosy sky, they all changed into smarter clothes and made their way to the restaurant car. It was a whole carriage full of tables with seats on either side and there were waiters with white coats whizzing around, carrying dishes of delicious-smelling food.

'How delightful,' said Grand-mère, as a waiter seated them.

Grand-mère and Agnes studied the menu, while Violet looked around. At the far end of the carriage was a young man. From the back he looked very much like Ralph, but Violet wasn't entirely sure. She whispered her suspicion to Agnes.

'Looks like who?' Grand-mère asked.

'What are you two talking about?'

'Oh, nothing!' Violet replied. Then, in an undertone, she said to Agnes, 'We need to get him to turn around.'

Agnes gave her a nod, which was meant to convey, *I will sort it out,* and, before Violet could stop her, Agnes took Mr Ratty out of the Ratbag and put him on the floor.

'Oh no, my pet rat has escaped!' she cried, jumping to her feet, as Mr Ratty, unable to believe his luck, trundled off into the main aisle, weaving between the waiters' feet.

The effect was instant. Everyone started to shriek and climb on their chairs.

'Did that girl say RAT?'

'There it is! Over there!'

'I'm so sorry! Really I am!' Agnes cried, as she scampered after Mr Ratty, diving under tables, trying to catch him.

Grand-mère smiled graciously, as everyone shot her evil looks, which said, *I cannot believe you have let your granddaughter bring a RAT into the restaurant car.*

'Violet, go and help your cousin,' she hissed.

Mr Ratty was finally brought to a stop by an enormous piece of bread that had fallen on the floor, right by the table where the young man who looked like Ralph was sitting. He gave Agnes a horrified glance as she knelt to scoop the rat up.

'Oh, Mr Ratty, you are so naughty,' Agnes said, shoving him back in his bag.

'It is Ralph,' she whispered to Violet, as she sat down.

'Well done!' Violet whispered and, as the dining car settled down after Mr Ratty's escape, Violet fixed her eyes on Ralph. *He clearly wasn't excavating near the pyramids because he was on a train to Luxor. What was he up to? And with whom?*

But Ralph didn't give her any further clues. He ate his dinner and then got up and left the restaurant car.

Grand-mère, Violet and Agnes finished their meal and made their way back to their compartment. Grand-mère gave a couple of large yawns and announced she was ready for bed. They all changed into their pyjamas, washed their faces, cleaned their teeth, got into their berths and pulled out their books. Violet was reading *Pippi Longstocking*, which was one of her favourites, but she was finding it hard to concentrate. In fact, there was so much to think about it was making her brain hurt. Ralph must be going to the Valley of the Kings, but what was he excavating there? Agnes didn't think it was Nefertiti, so why all the secrecy? And why had Professor Fitzherbert wanted to keep the letter? To translate the hieroglyphs himself or because he didn't want them to? Either way, it was suspicious behaviour. There was a thud as Grand-mère, who had fallen asleep, dropped her book, and Violet decided to try to go to sleep too. Before she did, she stuck her head down to Agnes and said, 'We need to follow Ralph tomorrow to see where he goes. Do you think we should send Rose and Art to search Professor Fitzherbert's house in London?'

'That's a good idea. He was very strange about the letter,' Agnes agreed.

'I'll ring Rose in the morning from the station. I'll tell Grand-mère that she's competing in an important ballet competition and I want to wish her luck,' Violet said, yawning.

'Great plan and, while you do that, I'll keep an eye on Ralph,' Agnes replied. And, with the decision made, both girls fell asleep.

Rose was out at her ballet class when Violet phoned, so she rang Art instead. He agreed with her that it all sounded very fishy and that he would go and take a look at Professor Fitzherbert's house with Rose.

Violet went back to meet Agnes and Grand-mère in the taxi queue. She spotted Ralph just a few people in front of them.

'Oh, I am excited,' said Grand-mère, peering at her guidebook on the Valley of the Kings. 'I think we should start with the tomb of

Rameses IX and then . . .' She carried on, but the girls weren't listening. They were busy watching Ralph.

'Valley of the Kings, please,' they heard him say to a taxi driver.

'It should be easy to find him there,' Agnes whispered to Violet. 'We can ask one of the guides where the archaeologists are excavating and then go and see exactly what Ralph and Alf are up to.'

The queue moved quickly and they were soon climbing into a taxi themselves.

It was only a short ride to the Valley of the Kings and the taxi dropped them at the entrance. It was crowded with stalls selling souvenirs and ice cream, as well as with tourists and guides and . . .

'Donkeys!' Grand-mère gasped. 'How enchanting! I haven't ridden on one for years. We must hire some – but which ones?' she asked, surveying the donkeys and guides with a piercing gaze, like a commander eyeing her troops. Her eyes came to rest on a boy of about Violet and Agnes's age, who was standing with three donkeys, stroking their noses and talking to them. She strode over to him and began to negotiate, while Agnes and Violet tried to see if they could spot any signs of Ralph.

There were none, but Agnes did notice a policeman, sitting to one side of the crowds, on a small platform. He was engrossed in a book and Agnes gave a shriek of laughter.

'Look, Violet!' she said. 'Look what that policeman is reading!'

Violet looked, and then giggled too as she saw the familiar cover of *Solving Crime: The Green Way*.

'Let's go and ask him about excavations in the Valley,' Agnes suggested.

As the girls approached him, the policeman barely looked up from his book. They asked about excavations, but he just grunted about there being only one up by the tomb of Rameses IX.

He was so rude that Violet couldn't resist being a little cheeky. 'Thank you for your help,' she said. 'And, by the way, I do hope you're enjoying that book; it was written by a friend of mine.'

'What?' The book went down and the policeman was suddenly interested. 'You know Percival Green?'

'Yes, very well,' Violet replied.

'Oh, you are so lucky,' he sighed. 'He is amazing. I think he is quite the equal in intelligence and skills to the great Sherlock Holmes.'

Violet tried her best not to smile at the comparison.

'Violet! Agnes!' Grand-mère was calling them. 'Come here.'

'I am honoured to meet two friends of the wonderful PC Green. My name is Lieutenant Khouri and, if I can be of any assistance, please let me know.'

'This is Ahmed,' Grand-mère announced to

Violet and Agnes, as they walked over. 'He is going to be our guide. And these are his donkeys. Do they have names, Ahmed?'

'Yes, madam,' Ahmed replied. 'This is Donkey Number One – he is perfect for you.' Number One was sweet-looking with serious eyes and fluffy ears. He sat entirely still as Grand-mère hoisted herself onto him.

'Donkey Number Two is for you,' he said to Agnes, giving her a shy smile. He held the reins of a similarly nice donkey as Agnes got on.

'And Donkey Number Three is for you,' he said matter-of-factly to Violet, handing her the reins of the crossest donkey Violet had ever seen. 'You will have to show him who is boss.'

Great! thought Violet. Number Three fixed her with his beady eyes and proceeded to trot away as she tried to get on him.

Ahmed tutted. 'You have to be tough with him.' And he gave a sharp tug on the reins, which brought the donkey to a halt.

'Thank you,' Violet replied.

'Now, please can you take us to see Rameses IX first?' Grand-mère asked.

'Of course,' Ahmed said. 'Come on, let us go.' He gave Donkey Number One a gentle pull and led him off. Agnes's donkey trotted obediently behind, but Violet's refused to move.

'Oh, come on, Number Three,' she said, gently kicking him in the sides, as she would a horse. He still wouldn't move so she kicked him a little harder and he shot off like a rocket, nearly throwing her off.

Ahmed laughed when he saw them. 'That donkey has the soul of a racehorse,' he said.

9
SOMETHING IS WELCOMED TO THE WORLD

As Lieutenant Khouri had said, next to the tomb of Rameses IX was an excavation.

'Grand-mère, I think some friends of ours might be working on that dig – can we go and say hello?' Violet asked, as they all climbed down from the donkeys.

'Very well,' Grand-mère replied. 'Don't be too long though. Meet me in the tomb in ten minutes.' She went off, clutching her guidebook, while Ahmed looked after the donkeys.

The area was shut off by a sign saying

MUSEUM OF CAIRO
NO ENTRY

but Agnes, who had been on plenty of digs with her parents, was used to signs like that. Ignoring it, she led them forward.

'Hi, Agnes, what are you doing here?' a friendly voice called, and a woman appeared.

'Hi, Mona,' Agnes replied. 'I'm just visiting the Valley with my grandmother and my cousin, Violet. This is Mona,' she explained to Violet. 'She's my mum's boss. Mona, we're looking for two men from the British Museum – Alf or Ralph? Have you seen them?' she asked.

Mona shrugged. 'I'm sorry but no – there's only me and two of my assistants from the museum in Cairo.'

'That's strange,' Agnes said. 'Is there another excavation in the Valley?'

'No, definitely not,' Mona replied. 'Sorry not to be able to help. Would you like to come and see these wall paintings that we've just found?'

Agnes and Violet exchanged confused glances. Where on earth could Ralph be?

'We'd love to, but we promised our grand-mère we wouldn't be long. Perhaps if we have time later we can come back?' Agnes said.

'I don't understand it,' Violet said, as they made their way back to the tomb. 'The letter said that he was returning to the excavation today and we even saw Ralph take a taxi here from the station. He must be in the Valley somewhere.'

'I wish I could work out these hieroglyphs,' Agnes said, pulling the letter out of her pocket. 'I'm sure it's a massive clue.'

TO THE WORLD!

LOVE, RALPH

'Ah, there you two are,' said Grand-mère, who was standing by the donkeys, having just finished looking round the tomb. 'Ahmed and I were wondering where you had got to. It's time to go and see the tomb of Tutankhamun!'

Violet had been so excited about seeing Tutankhamun's tomb, but now all she could think about was what Ralph and Alf were up to. She tried to shake off the feeling she was missing something as the three of them made their way down into the burial chamber. Agnes read the guidebook while Violet and Grand-mère looked at the mummy of the boy king. He had the same other-worldly expression as Matilde's mummy, Tey.

'He was only eighteen years old when he died, you know,' said Grand-mère. 'Some people think that he was killed in a chariot race—'

'OH!' Agnes exclaimed suddenly.

'What is it?' Grand-mère asked with alarm.

'Um . . . nothing. I thought I saw a spider.' Grand-mère tutted and turned back towards the mummy.

'Look, those five symbols for beauty that we couldn't work out,' Agnes whispered to Violet, pointing at a picture of hieroglyphics in the guidebook. 'They're part of Nefertiti's name!!'

'Really? So what does letter say?' cried Violet, as Agnes pulled it out of her pocket.

'Welcome Nefertiti to the world!'

Violet gasped. 'So they *are* excavating Nefertiti's tomb! And that means that it was Ralph and Alf who stole the mummy!'

'We need to find them and stop them!' Agnes cried.

'But how when we don't know where they'll be excavating?' Violet said.

'The Valley is pretty small,' Agnes replied.

'We should be able to find them.'

Before Violet had a chance to answer, the girls saw Grand-mère approaching.

'Shall we tell her?' Agnes whispered. 'Perhaps I should ring Mama and tell her too? Or maybe I should go and tell Mona . . .'

'No, or at least not yet,' Violet decided. Everything always became slower and more complicated when grown-ups got involved.

'Isn't it just fascinating, girls?' Grand-mère said. 'I think we should go and see the tomb of Tuthmosis IV next.'

They set off on their donkeys, with Number Three still behaving atrociously, but Violet was so busy looking for evidence of excavations and thinking everything through that she hardly noticed. She couldn't believe that they hadn't been more suspicious of Ralph and Alf back in London. They reached the next tomb and, although it was very interesting, there was no sign of any excavation.

'We haven't been to that part of the Valley yet so we should look there next,' Agnes whispered to Violet, pointing southwards.

'Grand-mère, can we go and see Amenhotep II?' she asked.

'Of course,' Grand-mère replied. 'I think that that will have to be the last tomb we see though – we need to get to the station in good time for the train back to Cairo this afternoon.'

'Oh no!' both girls chorused. They were so close; to go back to Cairo now with nothing solved would be unbearable. *If the excavation isn't down here,* Violet said to herself, *then we'll tell Grand-mère and Mona, and maybe go* and find that policeman, *Lieutenant Khouri*. *If we explain everything to them, they're sure to help.*

'Well, girls,' Grand-mère said, 'I'm delighted that you are so enthusiastic about sightseeing, but I'm afraid we do need to get back.'

Ahmed led them along the path down the centre of the Valley, but Number Three soon decided to go off in another direction and this time he picked a narrow track that climbed steeply up the side of the Valley.

'Number Three, you are so annoying!' Violet cried, as Grand-mère, Ahmed and Agnes waved cheerily at her from the valley below, laughing, as they got off their donkeys and disappeared into the tomb.

The path was much too narrow to turn the donkey around so Violet just had to sit and wait as it led her up and up. When they reached the brow of the hill, the path opened out before it dropped into the valley beyond. Violet seized her chance and, taking hold of the reins sharply, she tried to turn Number Three around. But this seemed to infuriate the donkey and he set off at a gallop down the path into the next valley. Violet clung on for dear life. Then the path swung sharply round the corner and Violet caught her breath.

For there, below, was a van, a couple of tents, and the unmistakable figures of Ralph and Alf. They both jumped as the donkey thundered towards them and came to a sharp stop, sending Violet flying.

'Well, well, what do we have here?' Ralph called. 'Dad, you'd better come and see what the donkey dragged in!'

10
NO MERCY

It was only after putting down the telephone to Violet that Art realised he didn't have Professor Fitzherbert's address. He rang PC Green, who spent a long time flicking through various notebooks, before announcing, 'Nope, sorry, Art, I never took the address down.'

'How else can we find out his address?' Art asked. 'Would Dolores have it?'

'Good thinking. Hold on a minute, I'll just go and check.'

He returned a minute later.

'Clever Dolores has it. She says she's busy just at the moment, but why don't we all go together later? Shall we pick you up about four? It'll be a fun outing – I'll bring snacks!'

It was nearly dark by the time they found Professor Fitzherbert's house. It was on the edge of Richmond Park, and was large and ancient-looking. Rose thought it looked more like a museum or a grand house in the country. They had hoped the house would be empty so they could have a snoop around, but as they drove towards it they saw the lights were on and a woman was drawing curtains across the huge first-floor windows.

'That's Miss Beasley!' Rose cried.

'What is she doing here?' PC Green said.

'Perhaps she's looking after the house for the Professor while he's away?' Art suggested.

'Hmm,' Rose said, thinking hard. 'We always thought Miss Beasley was involved with Professor Petit, but maybe we've got the wrong Professor.'

'Since the theft of the mummy is your case, why don't you go and ask Miss Beasley if you can look around the house?' Dolores suggested to PC Green. 'Remember to be very charming as we don't have a warrant so she doesn't have to let you in.'

PC Green pulled what he thought was his most charming face, but actually just made him look peculiar.

'Er, on second thoughts, just be your normal delightful self,' Dolores said hurriedly.

'Shall I come too?' suggested Art, thinking that PC Green might be so busy sucking up to Miss Beasley that he'd forget to look for clues.

'Good plan,' Rose said quickly, thinking the same thing.

'And, while she's busy showing you two around, Rose and I will take a look at the garden, just to see if there's anything suspicious there,' Dolores said.

They parked the car and, as Rose and Dolores hid behind a hedge, PC Green and Art walked along the crunchy gravel drive and rang the doorbell. After a short conversation, Miss Beasley let them into the house, shutting the door behind them, and Dolores and Rose scooted round the side of the house, into the garden.

Professor Fitzherbert's garden was large and

spooky and full of huge bushes that loomed out of the dark. Rose went in one direction and Dolores in the other.

At the far end of the garden, Rose found a small hill that seemed to be covered with big potholes. *How strange!* she thought to herself, as she walked up it and down the other side.

There was a high hedge at the bottom, with a narrow gap in it, like the entrance to a maze. Curious, she walked through it, only to find the ground disappear beneath her feet. Poor Rose fell down and down, before landing with a thump on her bottom.

'Ow!' she cried, but after a quick check she found that her bottom was the only bit of her that hurt, and it was recovering fast. *Where am I?* she wondered, looking around.

Rose was in a large, deep hole, hidden from the rest of the garden by the hedge. In front of her was a ladder, leading back up to ground level, and, behind her, a grand doorway. Walking towards it, Rose felt her foot touch a soft, squidgy button in the floor and a small light came on above the doorway, illuminating it. The doors were made of dark metal and had pictures of pyramids and hieroglyphs engraved on them.

Above her, Rose heard Dolores's concerned voice call: 'Rose? Are you all right?'

'I've found the entrance to something,' Rose replied.

Dolores climbed down the ladder to join her.

'Mmm, interesting,' she said, inspecting the doors. 'There's no door handle.'

'There's a keypad,' Rose said, pointing to a small panel by the door. 'Perhaps that opens the door?'

'But we don't have the number,' Dolores said with a sigh. She was turning to go when the doors slid open with a hiss.

'That's strange,' Rose said.

'It is,' Dolores replied and paused. 'Well, we might as well go in.' And they stepped through the doors.

As soon as they did, the doors shut behind them and they found themselves squashed together in a tiny lobby, staring at another set of lift-like doors. Just as Rose was beginning to feel anxious, the doors opened, and Rose and Dolores walked into a large room with a domed ceiling.

It was like entering a room at the British Museum, with its stone floor and display cases of carefully labelled artefacts. And in the centre, like Snow White in her glass coffin, lay the stolen mummy.

'I don't believe it!' Rose cried. 'It must have been Professor Fitzherbert all along!'

Dolores looked carefully at the display cases. 'Here are all the objects stolen from the museum too,' she said. 'There's no doubt about his guilt, but I wonder whether Miss Beasley is involved as well. We should go and see how the others are getting on in the house.'

Rose agreed and they walked back to the

entrance. The first set of doors opened obligingly and shut with a hiss as they walked into the lobby. They waited for the outer entrance doors to open, but nothing happened.

Dolores looked for a handle or a button or something. But there was nothing.

Then a trickling noise came from the floor and they looked down to see water seeping in by their feet. Just a little at first, but soon it began to gush in, quickly covering the toes of their shoes. A few minutes later, it was up to their ankles.

'What's going on?' Rose cried.

At that moment, Professor Fitzherbert's voice boomed from a speaker above them.

'No mercy is shown to robbers and thieves!'

'It's a trap!' Dolores cried.

'Let us out! Let us out!' they both shouted, hammering on the doors as the water crept up their legs.

11
CRYING NEVER HELPS

'Oh, why won't you listen to advice, Violet? I told you to forget about solving the crime, and yet here you are, sticking your nose in!' Professor Fitzherbert said, as he towered over her. Then he pulled her up by the scruff of her neck and marched her towards the hillside and through a narrow opening in the rocks.

Ralph smacked Number Three hard on its bottom and the donkey bolted back up the path.

'I can't believe that you've been stealing from

the museum that you run!' Violet spluttered.

'I don't like to think of it as stealing. I prefer to view it as moving objects from one collection to another more exclusive one, where they can't be gawped at by a load of good-for-nothing, snotty-nosed children who have no proper understanding of what they're looking at.'

'But you've sabotaged Matilde's research!' Violet cried.

'No I haven't. I've finished it off for her,' he said, and dragged Violet through the tunnel until they came out into a large chamber, its walls covered in hieroglyphs.

'Welcome to the treasure chamber of Queen

Nefertiti's tomb,' he said. 'I have to say it was full of the most spectacular treasure I have ever seen. As you can see, we've emptied it and now it's all being loaded into the van outside, ready to go to Cairo.'

Despite the circumstances, Violet couldn't help but look around in wonder at the hieroglyphics and paintings.

'I suppose you're going to keep all the treasure for yourself?' Violet said, as the Professor shoved her onto the floor and roughly tied her hands behind her back, before doing the same with her feet.

'No, only the best bits. The rest I'll sell privately to other collectors.'

'Won't they care that it's stolen?'

'No, everyone will be much too delighted to ask questions. And tomorrow we blast through to the tomb itself. Dynamite is a little destructive, but oh so quick.'

Before Violet could tell him how awful, greedy and selfish he was, he pulled a handkerchief from his pocket. 'Quite clean, I assure you,' he said, and gagged Violet with it. 'That should keep you quiet until I decide what to do with you. Perhaps I'll leave you here for the jackals and the hyenas. They get terribly hungry at night.' And with that he left Violet all alone.

'I will not cry,' Violet said to herself, as two fat tears rolled down her cheeks. 'Crying never helps,' she added, but it was too late and she began to sob as best she could with a gag in her mouth.

'Oh dear, feeling sad, are we?' Professor Fitzherbert said, coming back into the tomb. 'Never mind, I've brought you some company.' And he flung Agnes on the floor next to Violet, before starting to tie Agnes up too. 'Sorry, not so clean,' he said, as he pulled another handkerchief - this one dirty and crumpled - out of his pocket and gagged her with it. 'Anyway, I must be off. I have some dynamite to prepare!'

Alone in the room, the two girls sat on the floor, feeling very sorry for themselves. But then, after about twenty minutes, they heard Grand-mère's familiar voice outside, talking to Professor Fitzherbert. *Yes!* Violet thought. *Grand-mère to the rescue!*

'My dear lady,' Professor Fitzherbert was saying, oozing charm. 'I am so sorry that you have lost your granddaughters. How very distressing for you. I can assure you that we have not seen them.'

'Hmm,' Grand-mère said. There was something about Professor Fitzherbert that she didn't trust. He hadn't mentioned that he was coming to the Valley of the Kings at tea the day before. *But then why would he lie about Violet and Agnes?* she asked herself.

'Very well, thank you for your help. Come, Ahmed, we will try the other path. Or perhaps they have gone back to the main entrance . . .'

Inside the tomb, Violet and Agnes looked at each other in despair as they heard Grand-mère leave.

12
A FIGURE LOOMS

Back in London, Art and PC Green were driving away from Professor Fitzherbert's house. PC Green had just been summoned away on urgent police business, and Art didn't want to alert Miss Beasley to Rose and Dolores's presence, so he was pretending to leave with PC Green. Miss Beasley hadn't been exactly welcoming, but, after a bit of persuasion, she had given them a full tour of the house. They had found no trace of the mummy, though it quickly became clear that Miss Beasley, Ralph, Alf and Professor Fitzherbert knew each other rather well.

In fact, you could say *extremely* well, since they were clearly a family and the house was full of photos of the four of them. *Why would they not mention that at work?* Art wondered, thinking how suspicious it was, and even PC Green thought it was a little strange. He asked Miss Beasley why they had kept it a secret.

'The boys and I wouldn't want anyone thinking that we got our jobs because of Archie,' she replied.

'But you did,' PC Green replied, puzzled.

Miss Beasley was saved from having to answer this by PC Green's radio crackling into life and a cross voice saying, 'Green, where are you?! You're supposed to be keeping order at the dog walkers' protest in the park. Apparently, it's getting dangerously out of hand!'

'Sorry, Sergeant, I'll be there in a jiffy,' he replied. 'Right, must dash. Thank you for your co-operation, Miss Beasley.'

Just then an alarm went off in the house. Miss Beasley gave a start and said, 'Oh dear, not again. The alarm's been playing up all day. If you'll excuse me, I'd better sort it out.'

'Of course,' PC Green said. 'You don't want

the police turning up or anything annoying like that,' he added jokingly.

'How funny you are!' Miss Beasley said, as she ushered them out of the front door. As soon as they were gone, she ran to her laundry room and pulled back the wooden screen of pretend cupboards to reveal a bank of television screens that were linked up to the many cameras that covered the house and, most importantly, their priceless collection of artefacts.

'Oh dear, who's snooping?' she said to herself, as she saw Rose and Dolores standing outside the entrance to the collection. She paused as she decided what to do.

She couldn't have them alerting PC Green now, so she would let them into the collection and deal with them once she was sure that the policeman had left. She pressed a button and the doors slid open for them. She watched as they walked into the domed room and then turned her attention back to PC Green and Art. A camera showed them walking out of the gate.

'Well, that's got them out of the way,' she said to herself and, as Rose and Dolores walked back into the small lobby, she pressed a few more buttons. She laughed meanly. 'Oh dear

 me, you do look hot - let's cool you down,' she said and

then switched on the water and the recorded message of her beloved husband booming, 'No mercy is shown to robbers and thieves!'

'Right, stop here,' Art said to PC Green, after they had driven a short way down the street. 'She'll have seen us leave on the camera.'

'Okay, but I don't know why you don't trust her,' PC Green said, stopping the car. 'She seems very nice to me. But then,' he added, in a rare moment of insight, 'whenever I think people are nice, they're usually crooks. Are you sure you'll be all right looking for the others on your own?'

Art reassured him that he would be and

they said goodbye. Art walked back towards the house and, to avoid the cameras, he clambered over the railings into the park. He skirted round the high garden walls. It wasn't easy, but eventually he found a place to climb over into Professor Fitzherbert's garden.

Despite the night being very dark, when Art got into the garden, he found that he could see rather well, because the 'hill' that Rose walked over was, in fact, the domed roof of the collection, and the 'potholes' were several small glass windows, out of which light was now pouring. Art immediately scooted over to them and the first thing he saw was the mummy staring right back at him.

He rushed to the next roof light and then the next, desperately looking for Rose and Dolores. He was about to give up and look elsewhere when he reached the last roof light and saw a terrible sight. Rose and Dolores were trapped in a tiny space with water up to Dolores's waist and Rose's chest. He couldn't hear them, but could tell from their expressions that they were screaming and shouting. Art looked around desperately for something he could use to smash the glass. But then he gave a gasp and froze, as he saw a figure walking across the garden towards him.

In the tomb, Agnes was making faces at Violet and bending down as if she was trying to reach something, but Violet couldn't work out what on earth she was doing. And then, in a flash, she realised.

The Ratbag.

She could see it was slightly open and Mr Ratty was poking his nose out.

But Violet couldn't see what use he was likely to be, or how she was supposed to open the bag with her hands and feet tied and her mouth gagged, which left her with her . . . nose? There was no way Violet was putting her nose anywhere near Mr Ratty. Perhaps she could use her chin? Since there were no other options, Violet shuffled towards him.

With Agnes's encouragement and much manoeuvring, Violet found herself lying awkwardly on the floor, trying to shunt the zip along with her chin as Mr Ratty gently nudged her with his teeth. Violet tensed, waiting for him to sink his teeth in at any moment. But he resisted the temptation and, after a few attempts, she managed to slide the zip open enough for the rat to jump out. Violet quickly sat up again as she heard footsteps approaching.

Professor Fitzherbert entered the room. 'We will soon be leaving for Cairo, so toodle-pip,' he said. 'We may see you in the morning, depending on how starving those hyenas I mentioned are. Of course there are also the scorpions and snakes . . . Oh look, there's a rat to keep you company!' He chortled. 'So long, girls.'

There is nothing like talk of being eaten by hyenas to focus the mind and Agnes desperately began trying to coax Mr Ratty to chew the ropes behind her back. It looked unlikely to work at first, but after the rat had discovered that there was nothing else to eat, he began to gnaw obligingly on Agnes's ropes. In a few minutes, they were loose enough for Agnes to slip her hands out and she was able to free her feet and pull off the gag. Agnes turned her attention to Violet and freed her too.

'We must stop them before they go!' Agnes whispered. 'We can't let them escape with all Nefertiti's treasure.'

Violet nodded. 'We need a plan,' she said. 'There are three of them and only two of us. Let's see what they're doing.'

Agnes looked for Mr Ratty to put him back

in his bag, but he had disappeared.

'Oh no!' she cried.

'He'll turn up later,' Violet said confidently. They had more important things to worry about than an adventurous rat.

The girls crawled silently on their stomachs to the entrance of the tomb. Ralph and Alf were busy packing up the last of the tents. Professor Fitzherbert was nowhere to be seen.

'If only one of us could drive!' Agnes sighed in exasperation.

'I can, sort of,' Violet replied and, when Agnes looked amazed, she quickly explained about her father and godfather teaching her on

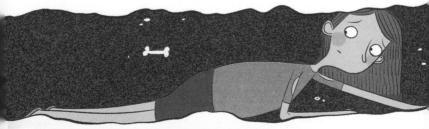

their holiday in Dorset. Agnes was extremely jealous.

'I'll get them to teach you too,' Violet said. 'But, for now, could you distract Ralph and Alf while I try to get to the van?'

'Of course,' Agnes replied. 'I will absolutely destroy them.'

And before Violet could tell her to wait until they both had their backs turned, Agnes had launched herself at Ralph and Alf with a Tarzan-like war cry. Alf and Ralph did look rather taken aback as Agnes spun around them like a whirling dervish, doing her kung-fu moves.

Wow, Violet thought, as she watched Agnes

topple them like bowling skittles. *She really is a lethal weapon.* Violet made a dash for the car and yanked the door open, jumping into the driving seat. She turned the key in the ignition and started the engine. Remembering Johnny's instructions, she put one foot on the brake and the other on the clutch, and then slammed it into first gear, released the handbrake and set off along the dirt track as fast as she could, speeding away from the camp. Looking in the rear-view mirror, she laughed out loud to see the twins lying on the floor, rubbing their heads in bewilderment, while Agnes danced around them, her hands and feet shooting out.

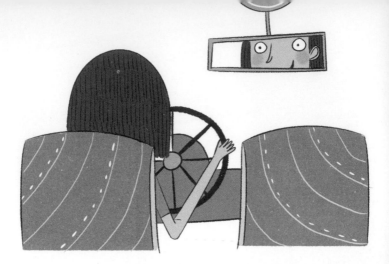

Violet could see a road ahead of her, which she was sure was the main road back to the entrance to the Valley of the Kings. If she could just reach it then she'd be able to find her way back and alert Grand-mère or Lieutenant Khouri.

'I've nearly done it!' she shouted with delight.

'Um no, I'm afraid you haven't,' a familiar voice said, and Violet froze, as Professor

Fitzherbert's face appeared in the rear-view mirror. He must have been in the back of the van all along! 'I think we'd better head straight back to camp, don't you?' And, reaching over her shoulder, he took the wheel and steered the van in the direction it had come from.

They were back in a moment. Violet felt like crying with frustration and disappointment.

14
A PLUMBING PROBLEM

The figure loomed over Art.

'After all that fuss, the Sarge sent someone else! I came back to see if you'd found the others,' PC Green said.

Art didn't think he had ever been so relieved to see anyone in his whole life.

'Rose and Dolores are trapped down there with water pouring in!' he cried. 'Here, give me your truncheon and I'll try and smash the glass.'

PC Green gave it to him and Art began to pound on the glass. PC Green looked over his shoulder.

'Blimey, it doesn't look much fun in there, does it?'

Art wasn't listening. As hard as he tried to break the glass, he didn't even make the smallest crack.

'Hmm, toughened glass,' PC Green said.

Art threw down the truncheon in frustration. 'We'll have to try and stop the water another way.'

'Why don't I go and tell Miss Beasley that she's got a plumbing issue - perhaps it's a blocked drain? Look, I can see her in her laundry room,' PC Green said, pointing to a window. 'She's got a lot of televisions in there. Do you think she watches them while she's doing the washing? What a good idea . . .'

Art was about to tell PC Green to stop being so utterly stupid and that it was Miss Beasley who was trying to drown poor Rose and Dolores, but then he realised that she must be controlling the water from that room and a plan formed in his mind.

'No, don't tell her she's got plumbing problems. Go and tell her that there's an emergency about Professor Fitzherbert.'

PC Green looked puzzled. 'But there isn't.'

'I know, but I need you to distract her.'

PC Green opened his mouth to object, but Art cut him off.

'Please, just trust me! Ring the doorbell until Miss Beasley answers and then keep her talking as long as you can, while I break into the laundry room and turn the water off.'

Art picked up the truncheon and ran towards the house, dodging from bush to bush, to avoid being seen. He crouched beneath the window sill of the laundry, so that he could see Miss Beasley, but she couldn't see him. Art heard the doorbell ring; at first Miss Beasley ignored it and then PC Green shouted through the letterbox.

'Miss Beasley, I know you're in there! It's an

emergency – it's about Professor Fitzherbert!'

Miss Beasley hesitated and then went to answer the door.

That was the moment Art had been waiting for. Using the truncheon, he smashed a pane of glass, which, to his relief, broke easily, and opened the window, climbing into the room.

An array of levers and buttons greeted him, none of which were labelled. He began to press them all in the hope that one would stop the water.

'What do you think you're doing?' Miss Beasley's furious face appeared in the doorway. 'Stop it this instant!' She grabbed Art's hands and wrenched them away from the buttons.

'I'm trying to release my friends before they drown!' he shouted at her.

'Thieves deserve to drown!' Miss Beasley cried.

'You're the thief, not them! You and Professor Fitzherbert stole the mummy from the museum in the first place.'

'Nonsense, we just removed it to our private collection so that it could be looked after properly.'

'I'm not sure the police would see it that way, madam,' PC Green said sternly, climbing in through the open window. Miss Beasley had slammed the door in his face when it became clear to her that there was no emergency with Professor Fitzherbert.

'Now, please release this young man and shut off the water.' PC Green started to press the buttons too.

'NO!' Miss Beasley hissed, launching herself at PC Green like a furious cat. There was a brief tussle and Miss Beasley sent PC Green flying across the room. As he fell to the floor, his hands reached out to grab what they could and he pulled hard on a lever. There was a sound of gushing water outside and shouts of relief from

Dolores and Rose.

The two of them appeared at the window, looking wet and bedraggled, and Miss Beasley looked like she would explode with fury.

'Right, Miss Beasley,' PC Green said, unlocking his handcuffs. 'I think you'd better come with me, don't you?'

15
Mr Ratty's Revenge

'Oh, for goodness' sake, you two! Can't you even cope with a little girl?' Professor Fitzherbert roared when he found Ralph and Alf rubbing their wounds.

Agnes had disappeared.

'Well, there's no time to worry about her now – we need to leave for Cairo this minute! Get into the van while I tie this one up again,' he said, gesturing to Violet. He picked up some ropes and tied her wrists so tightly that it made Violet wince. 'Into the back of the van with you. We'll have to dump you somewhere along the way.'

Just as he was about to shove Violet in, there was a clatter of hooves and in cantered Grand-mère, looking rather magnificent, followed by Agnes and Ahmed and Lieutenant Khouri on the other donkeys.

'Ha!' Violet said triumphantly to Professor Fitzherbert, as she struggled to get free from him.

'Not so fast, young lady, you haven't won yet,' he replied, holding her in a vice-like grip.

'Professor!' Grand-mère roared. 'Untie my granddaughter this instant!'

'Monsieur, I demand to see what is in that van!' Lieutenant Khouri cried.

Professor Fitzherbert put on his most charming voice. 'Sir, my dear lady—' he began.

'Don't you "my dear lady" me!' Grand-mère bellowed. 'Release Violet immediately!'

'Yes, let me go, you horrible man!' Violet shouted at him, trying to kick his ankles.

But Professor Fitzherbert held her tight.

'I'm afraid that Violet stays with me,' he said in a matter-of-fact tone. 'Now, just let us leave and no one will get hurt.' And he started to drag a furious, squirming Violet towards the van.

'Unhand that child!' Lieutenant Khouri

cried, reaching for his gun.

Professor Fitzherbert laughed. 'What are you going to do? Shoot me? I don't think so; you might hit this *poor little girl*. Face it, you've lost. Goodbye!'

They had nearly reached the van and, despite her ferocious struggling, Violet felt as if there was no escape, when suddenly something leaped through the air, landing on the Professor's face.

'AARGH!' Professor Fitzherbert cried, as Mr Ratty fastened his two front teeth firmly round the Professor's long, elegant nose.

Delighted, Violet elbowed him hard in the ribs and the Professor let go of her as he tried

to   pull
Mr   Ratty
off,   screaming   in
pain. Violet ran away as
fast as she could, but, before anyone could stop
her, Agnes sprinted towards the Professor.

'Don't you hurt my rat!! I am a lethal
weapon!' she cried, taking hold of his jacket
and pushing him over.

Ralph and Alf, seeing what was going on,
sped off in the van, spraying everyone in a
cloud of sand.

'Do not worry, they will not get very
far,' Lieutenant Khouri said, and then spoke

quickly into his radio.

Professor Fitzherbert lay on the floor, still grappling with Mr Ratty.

'Let go of my rat, you brute!' Agnes cried, kicking him.

Mr Ratty decided he had had enough of Professor Fitzherbert's nose, and gave his

fingers a quick nip to get him to loosen his grip, then jumped into Agnes's hands.

'Oh, you good boy!' she said, stroking him before she put him back in the Ratbag.

Quick as a flash, Lieutenant Khouri ran over and before the Professor knew what had happened he was in handcuffs.

'Oh dear, Professor Fitzherbert,' Violet said gleefully. 'It looks like you're the one who has lost now.'

After

Six months later, Rose, Violet, Art and Agnes stood proudly to one side of the large blue ribbon that would soon be cut to signal the opening of the British Museum's new blockbuster exhibition, 'The Lost Treasure of Queen Nefertiti'. It was already a sell-out and camera crews from all over the world were there to film the great event.

Despite Ralph and Alf trying to make a quick getaway with the treasure, Lieutenant Khouri's colleagues had caught up with the van before they reached Cairo. Along with Miss Beasley and Professor Fitzherbert, they had stood trial in London for stealing the mummy and in Cairo for excavating Nefertiti's tomb without permission. Found guilty on all counts, they had been sent to prison for a very long time. The newspapers were full of the story, and Mr Ratty was the star.

RAT-NAPPED!!

At the exhibition opening, Matilde, Professor Petit, Benedict, Camille, Grand-mère, PC Green, Dee Dee and Dolores were all in the audience. Mona, whom Violet and Agnes had met in the Valley of the Kings, had decided that she would like to spend a few years in London, so had applied to be the new Head of the Museum when Professor Fitzherbert was sent to jail, and much to everyone's delight she had been appointed. The even better news was that Mona and Professor Petit got on like a house on fire. Poor Professor Petit had been very upset to discover that Miss Beasley was, in fact, Mrs Fitzherbert and also found it very hard when Matilde got lots of attention for being responsible for finding Nefertiti's tomb. But working with Mona was definitely helping him feel much better. And now, as part of the opening, Mona was giving a wonderful speech.

'And so it is time to open the exhibition,' she said. 'I would like to give the honour of cutting the ribbon to the four friends without whom it would not have happened. It was their cleverness and courage that stopped Professor Fitzherbert and his family from stealing all this treasure and made sure that everyone can enjoy it.'

The audience applauded and cheered as Mona handed the scissors to Agnes.

Agnes took the scissors, but instead of cutting the ribbon she passed them to Rose.

'I think that Rose should open the exhibition, because she showed, as always, exceptional bravery,' Agnes said.

'Thank you,' Rose replied, a blush creeping over her face. She cut the ribbon, saying, with a grin to the others, 'Welcome Nefertiti to the world!'

The following day, Rose, Violet and Art sat on a bench in the communal garden. It was autumn, and the garden was bathed in mellow orange sunshine, and the lawn was littered with golden leaves. The three friends had met up to talk about their plans for Halloween, but had ended up discussing the theft of the mummy instead.

'We should have worked out who the thieves were sooner,' Violet said. 'We were too taken in by Professor Fitzherbert's charm.'

'We did miss some really obvious clues,' Art said.

'Like the fact that Miss Beasley and the twins started work at the museum at the same time as Professor Fitzherbert,' Rose said.

'And we should have investigated Miss Beasley's empty flat more,' Violet said.

'Oh well, we'll have to learn that lesson for next time,' Art said.

'Do you think there'll be a next time? Do you think there'll be another crime to solve?' Rose asked.

'Oh yes,' Violet replied confidently. 'In fact, I feel almost sure of it.'

Violet's extra-helpful word glossary

Violet loves words, especially if they sound unusual, so some of the words in her story might have been a little tricky to understand. Most of them you probably know, but Violet has picked out a few to explain . . .

Egyptology – the study of everything to do with life in Ancient Egypt

Archaelogist – a person who studies what life was like for people who lived in the past, usually more than a thousand years ago. Archaeologists often spend a lot of time on 'digs', which is when they are carefully digging in the ground looking for objects or buildings from the past.

Budding – you might be described like this when you are beginning to do something and are keen and getting good at it. For example, Violet, Rose and Art are 'budding' detectives.

Amulet – a piece of jewellery which is supposed to bring good luck

Culprit – the person who has committed the crime

Galavanting – wandering around

Whirling Dervish – when you twirl around like a spinning top

Ferocious – fierce

Gleefully – happy

BOOK LIST AND AUTHOR'S NOTE

There are many amazing books on Ancient Egypt, but the ones which were particularly useful to me were:

DK Eyewitness Project Book on Ancient Egypt by Jen Green. Published by DK 2009.

Egyptworld by Stella Caldwell. Published by Carlton Kids.

How to Read Egyptian Hieroglyphs by Mark Collier and Bill Manley. Published by the British Museum Press 2014.

The British Museum is a place I love and was a great inspiration to me in writing the story, but I did make up the details such as the Professor's door so please don't go looking for it!

HAVE YOU SOLVED THE OTHER VIOLET MYSTERIES?